Travel

Christine Brooks

AuthorHouse™
1663 Liberty Drive
Bloomington, IN 47403
www.authorhouse.com
Phone: 1 (833) 262-8899

Because of the dynamic nature of the Internet, any web addresses or links contained in this book may have changed
since publication and may no longer be valid. The views expressed in this work are solely those of the author and do
not necessarily reflect the views of the publisher, and the publisher hereby disclaims any responsibility for them.

Any people depicted in stock imagery provided by Getty Images are models,
and such images are being used for illustrative purposes only.
Certain stock imagery © Getty Images.

This book is printed on acid-free paper.

ISBN: 978-1-7283-6975-4 (sc)
ISBN: 978-1-7283-6976-1 (e)

Library of Congress Control Number: 2020914835

Print information available on the last page.

Published by AuthorHouse 08/27/2020

authorHOUSE®

I was seated on the airplane next to a well dressed distinguished gentleman. I couldn't tell his age, I kept my head tucked into my novel which was more interesting. He seemed very businesslike, unlike me the jeans and sneakers type, eventhough this is what I could afford. He seemed busy in thought therefore I did not disturb him.

This was my first visit to Denmark, therefore I was very excited, but I was alone, therefore I was keen on holding on to my purse and my valuables. I found out only a few people spoke English. I had my plans what I wanted to see. The major sights, the ancient buildings, the food, the people were all new to me. I never in million years dreamed this was what my trip would have turned out to be like.

By the way, I was seated by the window, and I always enjoy lift off. It's when I view gravity at its best. I watch the airplane speedup until it touches the air, from the ground to the air. That's my little secret now you know. Then it's time to relax and read. I thought the gentleman next to me was reading over my shoulder, then I thought no couldn't be naïve, that's my middle name.

I peeked through the window to take a look at the clouds, and the sky, with the sea beneath. And I thought to myself one day I will paint a portrait of it.

At some point on the trip I decided to take a break from my book and have a conversation with this stranger sitting next to me. He stated that he lived in Denmark but he went on a trip to N.Y. I smiled because he didn't seem like someone from Denmark he seemed like a native New Yorker. At this point I thought he was hiding his identity, however I decided to watch but I said nothing.

I thought I would go back to my novel but to my surprise my distinguished gentleman pulled out a gun and demanded that we turn the airplane around we are being hijacked, and he demanded that we go to a secluded area. I thought my heart was going to fly through my mouth. I said "Oh my God, what in heavens name is this". "Lord please don't let me die out here." Well what do you know there goes my well planned vacation, sight seeing and all. There were three other individuals working with him and we were told to remain calm, while the pilot turned the airplane around to a remote area. We landed in the middle of nowhere. I thought my life is crazy but this had taken it to new heights.

We were told to leave the airplane and we followed these orders. We were sent to a building where we were told there is someone very wealthy on the airplane and he was being held for ransome I thought well what does this have to do with me. I have my life and my plans. Why not hold him alone but we were told that we were all in this, therefore I said nothing. They called this persons family and demanded money or we would all be killed. And the gentleman stated one after the other would be killed.

My God I said this is not a very good situation I've gotten myself into this time around. They decided to have some people separated and have this person stay by himself. What a pickle I've gotten myself into this time around.

The people began freaking out and weeping. I had to remain calm and pray that our lives would be spared. Then then began to kill one set and this took a tole on everyone. I said "please let me speak to this guy's family so I could beg for my life and everyone elses." I told them "Look your son is still alive so please pay them so we can get back to our lives. Another set of people were transported off the island and to my surprise, God answers prayers, I was one of them. I was told if I ever repeat this to anyone I would be killed immediately.

Therefore I took my suitcase and left. I was very shaken but I was grateful for my life. I was told to resume life as if nothing happened. I landed in Denmark and went to my hotel, I thought I will just have to get some sleep. So I went to sleep but I couldn't help thinking about what just happened.

When I got up in the morning I decided to watch the news to see what was going on in the world. To my surprise it was a billionaire's son who was taken hostage and it was all over the news. I watched but I had to keep silent in order to keep my life.

I went to have lunch at my first restaurant in Denmark, I decided I will have to taste something new, so I could get the hijacking off my mind. I thought I would have to get something delicious, therefore I did. I enjoyed my meal and then went for a walk on the famous streets of Denmark. I began taking pictures and sketching the buildings. I had to try and enjoy my trip and since art always takes me to another world this is what I did.

Well since it was summer, I just had to take a look at the flowers and listen to the birds just to keep my sanity after what I had been through. I got up early in the morning, and took a morning stroll I marked the way to and from my hotel so that I find my way back. When I got back, I took my shower and headed for the stores to see if I wanted to shop for some new clothes. I decided to go window shopping, I picked up some souvenirs and then bought some slacks, sweats and tops. I felt a bit tired and therefore I headed home. I took a long hot shower and went to bed.

On the following morning I went out to the garden in the courtyard and the flowers were all arrayed in sets from the gardenias to the roses and the fragrance was intoxicating. I decided to take a stroll there. I went for breakfast and decided to have a relaxing cup of chamomile, and a bit to eat. I went back outside because I forgot the key to my room, when I got back someone took it therefore I had to get another set. When I opened the door, there stood my distinguished gentleman "Oh God!" I screamed not again. My life is spiraling out of control, and there is no one for me to share this with. He stated "remain calm", he would not hurt me. He came to find out if I had repeated what happened, I stated "no" and he left. I don't know how much longer I can keep up with this. I went to bed and that's it.

In the morning I decided to take a train ride and view the countryside. Therefore I took a shower, got dressed and headed for the train. I then got on the train and headed for just about any stop. I just wanted to breathe the fresh air and enjoy the view. I looked at the trees, the grass and the flowers. I had small talk with the people and their children. I took the train to the last stop and back. I enjoyed the ride immensely. It was then time for supper and a hot shower, some tea and bedtime. I turned in after a long and tedious but enjoyable day.

On the following day it rained heavily therefore I had a cup of chamomile and I decided to work on my labtop. I stayed in and had a relaxing day. I made plans for a tour, and searched the web for a reputable tour guide. I also looked at the news and slept for most of the day. I thought the rain would have help up a bit, but it didn't. I watched through the window as the rain fell. And I knew the flowers, trees and grass needed it. Therefore I just looked at the nature at its best. I decided to take the day off from everything, and make future arrangements for the following day.

I woke up to the sunshine coming through my windows, took my bath got dressed and headed outside. I had breakfast in a little café on the out skirts of Denmark. I then resumed painting the scenery of Denmark. I sat for about two hours and painted, then I began taking pictures of the people and nature. The buildings were so very different from N.Y. and so were the people. It was a sunny day therefore I enjoyed my time. I met a guy who told me he was also from N.Y. Good I finally met someone who had something in common with me, we both spoke English. He said he would be happy to show me around and we visited the countryside. His name was Gustav. We spent the evening together and after supper I went to bed and he went back to his apartment.

On the morrow Gustav and I went shopping for fruits, he wanted to show me the fruits in Denmark to see what I disliked. We then left and went into town to see a movie. We sat and talked about life and other interesting topics. I got to know him a little better, his likes and dislikes when we got through he went back to his apartment, but I decided to stay up and have tea with his sister who he introduced to me earlier.

We stayed up baking tarts and cookies for the children next door because they enjoyed this then we went to bed because we had a long day ahead.

In the morning Gustav came over to my apartment and we decided to go touring, we went to the flower shop to get flowers, then we left for the pool. He likes swimming and he decided to teach me how to swim. I was a bit shaky at first, because I did not want the water in my nose, but after a while I began to understand what to do. His sister Gustavia joined me with her son and her daughter, we all had fun at the pool. We took pictures of it all. Her daughter was 3rd yrs old at the time and her son seven. 3 yr old Naikla knows how to swim better than I do and I'm the adult. We all laughed together and enjoyed each others company. We stayed at the pool until 5pm when it was time to leave.

Gustavia went out Monday in order to get supplies for her house. On her way there a girl attacked her and pinned the blame on her. She lied and said Gustavia attacked her. Sharonique took Gustavia to court therefore I went with Gustavia for moral support.

The judge stated "On the date 15th of October 2007 the case of Sharonique vs Gustavia how does the defendant plead guilty or not guilty". Gustavia stated "Not guilty Your Honor". Her lawyer laid the foundation and stated "Gustavia attacked you, where are the bruises, at what time of the day did this occur, where are your witnesses, did you take pictures, were you hospitalized". Her answer to all this was no.

The cross examination even though she answered no to these key questions he has proof that this was true. Sharonique lied and her lawyer was working off all her lies. Therefore Gustavias lawyer said you have no case.

On the other hand, Gustavia had proof that it was Sharonique who attacked her. Her bruises were visible, the time of the day was 12 pm lunch time, she had witnesses and she took pictures and above all she had statements from the doctor at the hospital and her job, she had to take a month off. Her lawyer questioned her witnesses and they all gave the same answer.

We all waited for the court session to be over, and find out when would be the next court session. It was the next 5mths on March 2008.

Therefore we went to dinner, the lawyer said it was a good sign because she had no proof but Gustavia came prepared. We all sat up late and watched TV with the children. We stayed in the next day because we were tired from the previous activities.

Five mths passes and it was time to return to court. Sharonique did not show up therefore the session had to be rescheduled. Gustavia said "She knows she is lying", and we all went to the pool to have fun with the children. We stayed until closing time and then we had supper and stayed up and watched T.V..

Gustav had to get a new muffler for this car, and then we travelled to the north of town. We went to get a new project to work on for the children. We then visited their old school, where they met their friends, they always enjoyed this, therefore everyone was happy.

On Sunday we went to Church and Gustav and Gustavia gave their hearts to the Lord. We spent the evening together and exchanged numbers, because that Monday I was supposed to return home.

On Monday I boarded the airplane and said my goodbyes, the children were weeping but we told them that we would meet in NY when they got home. I left and went back home where I told my family what took place, I went back to work and school and resumed my life this was a trip I will never forget. The End.

Printed in the United States
By Bookmasters